# COMPRESSION

A Neophyte's Guide:
Explaining the Mystical Energies of
North and South America

Totukani Amen II

Inner Alchemy's Publishing
Chicago, IL

First Edition

ISBN 978-1-949432-01-5

Published by:

Inner Alchemy's Publishing, Inc.
332 S. Michigan Ave.
Ste 121-C141
Chicago, IL 60604-4434
info@inneralchemys.com
www.inneralchemys.com

Printed in the United States of America

# CONTENTS

# DISCLAIMER

# PREFACE

Speaking in reference to the common woman and man whom both are born into a world in which the first order seems to not know or question what is to be. Which in many cases it is not fault of their own not to be in the know. As if some sort of grand game is being placed between Gods spanning dimensions all to see what happens in every variation of circumstance.

As such, it is no longer going to be allowed for the fire that has been stolen from the Gods to wither away without at least an attempt from the Sages, Magi, Oracles, Sorcerer's, Witches, Super Human's, X- men/X-women, Meta-Humans and the like to move humanity forward in one way or another.

These are very special times in which the light of the minds eye of the individual is becoming ever brighter which shows passageways that are safer and easier to traverse. Take heed to this light and what it shows within the dark corners of not only the world, but yourself. Do not be afraid, in-fact know that many Masters have travelled before you and left crumbs on this yellow brickroad.

The only question is... will you accept your destiny?

# ACKNOWLEDGEMENTS

A toast to all the awakened beings
across the world whom are doing the great work
within themselves and without.

Whom regardless of their circumstances in life,
still persevere forever so.


Forward... forever forward.

# COMPRESSION

We will be discussing a bit on compression, and its counter expansion.

Neither is a positive nor a negative. And what this is dealing with is our compressed reality that many of us our within in one way or another, every day all day.

The problem is, if a problem exists, that is not understanding which you're in so you know how to operate accordingly. So, this can be taken somewhat as a manual, a short guide to the north American zones on planet earth. We will focus primarily on the United States and South America.

The United States itself could be looked at as a compression zone. Let us define compression via googles dictionary, and it states:

*Compression is*

*the action of compressing or being compressed.*

The reduction in volume (causing an increase in pressure) of the fuel mixture in an internal combustion engine before ignition.

As many have heard in one way or another that pressure can burst pipes, or make diamonds.

When one observes certain bacteria under a microscope, when they're put into compression, they tend to start to move faster, building colonies quicker than before as if in a rushed state. These microbial processes are all put in drive and the pedal is pressed down to the floor.

In our dimension, our reality, here in the United States, because this continent is under compression people especially in the past used to come here from all over the world to increase their current state or status in life. To better themselves, in most cases this was financially. They could come here and in a relatively short period of time against all odds, change the direction of their financial state forever.

The compression allowed them to move much faster, which provided more opportunities within that faster movement which may not even have been realized from whence they came. Their families are able to live out which what seems like a dream existence, watching within short periods of time their children growing to adulthood and achieving even more.

This would be a positive in compression.

As with love, when people love, they love intensely, deeply, and can even go so far into it that they become lost, in a good way.

If the sequences in positive change are made correctly, and in proper order, harmonious vibrations could easily take hold and move through the population bringing most into balance.

So, what would be a negative?

Well, as mentioned previously everything is under pressure, every-thing is moving faster. This includes everything from anger, violence, glut-tonous thoughts and actions and even hatred. People get angry and go from zero to one-hundred sometimes within a blink of an eye. And in this blink of an eye they either will cause physical harm or go off to conspire to cause harm later.

Decisions within compression are made much quicker, and many find themselves within circumstances where they have to make a choice im-mediately or an opportunity may be lost, forever. Everything within com-pression is exacerbated. And pushed to its extreme rather for positive or negative. This extreme will either make a diamond or burst a pipe.

Just as in the aforementioned positive example concerning the se-quences of positive change, the same in reverse can be made for negative.

For example, because many watch tv and believe all that they see, when a news anchor states that it's this group causing all the problems, or that group over there. It's the people with long beards, or people with

darker skin. Guess what happens? Whatever ideological difference has been pinned as the conspirer in the center of the sequence, then everyone focuses on that and it sweeps through the nation quicker than a blink of aneye.

Compression.

In compression there is no time to relax. You're always on the go. And even when relaxing, you're still on the move, rather this be physically, emotionally or mentally. In compression everything moves faster, which includes time. Are you keeping track?

Being stagnant within a compression zone means you will most definitely fall behind sooner or later.

Gate keepers in many cases are people trying to stop the progress of time. Wanting to keep things the same a bit longer, so they can pull a bit more from it. Sometimes this is a positive act but, in most cases, they're only wasting everyone else's time in the form of progress.

An example of progress within this time and space is concerning Dr. Delbert Blair and I. He knew something that only a few of you know about me and in that knowledge, he knew that the next step in progress could be made. A part of that is The Super-Human Trainings held all over the country where we dive deep into the universe, matrix, and most importantly the self. Yourself, myself, ourselves.

An example of potential stagnation is what occurred at Super Human Training Session 2. An elder stated, "I thought this was going to be like dr. Delbert Blair's lectures."

I asked, "What do you mean?"

She stated "Well, I like to sit back and just listen without needing to do anything and having some of the ideas Dr. Blair spoke on explained again"

I then stated, "I understand, and that's okay. But the next step in the progress of humanity, physically, mentally, emotionally and spiritually is going to require you, me, all of us to progress and do earnest work within self and that work may be difficult at times but if one requires that previous subjects be rehashed then they should go back and review previous lectures."

All in all, she said she understood, but she did not want to take that next step which has internal work required to raise her vibrations higher.

And that's is totally okay.

It required her to truly understand, innerstand and overstand what has come before and score at least an 80% on this hypothetical multi-dimensional test. Because the next steps are going to touch on new topics that address concerns and energy in the new age which Dr. Delbert Blair spoke on many times.

He was preparing humanity, those who will listen for this next step. And as that next step is engaged I'm now giving them a unique view which hasn't come before, showing proof, that even though I also live a human experience, what does an awakened being do during his or her life.

Super-humans, extraordinary men, women and children across the world, stand up! The universe has taken notice.

For others if you have watched all the historical lectures, broken all the codes of the universe but do not want to step further into the innerverse, guess what? That's is totally okay.

Just as there's nothing wrong with the elder knowing the level she rather reside. But in that, unless she does the bare minimum to stay equal within the compression zone, she will undoubtedly fall behind and potentially into hard times.

In compression you have to keep moving.

Within the United States the highest compression zones would be the northern states and the slowest compression zones would be the southern.

Because of this many in the north have stereotypes of those in the south, which many have heard of, that Southerners are slow in action, speech and thought. While Southerners have stereotypes of Northerners stating they talk and move to fast, can't be trusted and a bit shrewd.

These stereotypes exist for a reason and they're exposing an underlying truth about the reality we live in.

Just a side note before we get into expansion realities, compression realities could be looked at as the air kingdoms while expansion realities could be looked at as the earth kingdoms. Hence why in the current compression zones you will find higher technology and in the expansion zones you will find those who live closer to the ways of the earth.

Also, if compression is getting to you and you need a bit of help. Some advice I could give for those in compression to get ahead and lessen the load is to look into communal living. Ethnicities all over the world come to the United States and do just this for as long as it takes until the individual is able to flourish on his or her own without issue.

Many in compression turn into parasites as well, feeding on others and taking from everyone and everything as if a vampire feeding on the blood of its host. The reason for this is because they couldn't keep up with compression, fell back or began to fall back and so their energy inverts.

The tesseract, that hyper dimensional cube that produces the massive amount of energy within a human, that allows a human to move a 2 ton car with one hand under stress to save their child , falls back on itself causing a black hole. An emptiness that forever needs to be filled.

Based on observation as well as data sets obtained from the Census and other databanks it seems that those in Compression have very specific migration patterns.

For those who have lived in compression all of their life and even more so have lived in the highest compression zones such as Chicago or New York tend to move to the United States south. Those in the south tend to move even further south within the United States or to South America.

# EXPANSION

S outh America itself could be looked at as an expansion zone.

Let us define expansion via googles dictionary, and it states:

*Expansion is*
*a thing formed by the enlargement, broadening,*
*or development of something.*

*"Expand onward and conquer all, and put what thy sees under my dominion."*

Quote from some old guy in the air kingdom looking to rule over that which was beneath.

The expansion kingdoms of South America; the earth kingdoms in which the people typically live a perceived slower existence compared to their compressed counterparts. Typically, the people, practices and technologies are more aligned with the way the energy flows in these places verses making the place flow to you.

If you were born in expansion, your life was filled with outdoor activities, lots of exercise and being fine- tuned by the kingdom of earth. Your ways and values will be grounded within the realism of the reality around you. Typically, those in expansion understand and appreciate the great mother even if it's symbolically because they know where their food derives and if they abuse her, she will not bring forth what is needed as nourishment.

Unlike some who dwell within the air kingdoms, always within their minds, tinkering and creating new toys to be deployed.

The people in expansion, the strongest of them tending to be as strong and resilient as the ground they have walked on all of their life and equally as proud. Just ask those who were trained within the great rite of the jaguar. Songs are sang to this day, remembering those who were the children of the great mother and embodied her spirit to keep away all that were not welcome.

But just as in the air kingdom, which is the worlds of compression all is not positive nor negative. It's just the state of the current energy around us.

This energy is based on a few factors.

One being the current continents that are visible and not underwater. Even if you take into consideration that the great continent, mythically known as Pangea was broken and spread over the waters. Our current continent of North America has parts of her submerged. These portions underwater could indeed bring a bit more balance to these lands if they weren't submerged deadening their energetic signatures.

Many in compression venture to live within expansion when they get older in age. The reason for this is because with the coins they have gathered over their life time they are able to go much further. Life is much slower. They don't have to think all day every day what their next move will be, or be bombarded with the on-goings of air kingdom politics.

They can just sit outside of their beach house all day, until the sun sets.

But... As one could expect as more compressionist arrive, they change ever more slightly the energy of a given area. Changing into just another city of compression set within the background of expansion.

From the ever more businesses, regulations, and everything needing to be licensed.

"We need internet and cellular service," an air kingdom resident yells from within the crowd.

And so comes the bull dozers, air planes, cell phone towers, fine dining, and this is all plotted out with the clearing of the ancient forest, the jaguars home, pushing him further back into his sacred lands, ever watched over in silence waiting for a reply form the Quetzalcoatl.

Many from compressed realities have for decades been flocking to Panama, Costa Rica, Dominican Republic, Puerto Rico and many others cities and countries slowly carving out a distinct way of life for air kingdom residents.

"Ayyeee... Why not though, air kingdoms coins are worth much more!" Stated, by an unknown Earth Kingdom resident.

You will find many more compression zone citizens with expansion zones than expansion zone citizens within compression zones. For many the fast paced life style, the shrewdness, mental games, technology, and electromagnetic frequencies becomes too much for these earth kingdom citizens. And even if they stay in the compression for financial reasons, once goals our met they find their way back home.

You will also find that many from compression flock to the expansion to take advantage of those within the earth kingdoms. Since air kingdoms citizens tend to think faster, and move quicker than their earth kingdom counterparts this is utilized to their advantage to create cults and other types of massive followings.

To those from the earth kingdoms god came down from the heaven and taught them new ways both good and evil. And they were changed forever more.

When this is all said in done, in these times use this as a small guide so you can dwell where you need to, to accomplish whatever is in your heart.

Both kingdoms have pros to some while cons to others and that's okay.

# ADDITIONAL WORKS
# BY AUTHOR

## An Alchemist Journey in Scent
### Author's Life Story

# ADDITIONAL WORKS
# BY AUTHOR

## Book I–Lessons
Karma Release and Internal Power Generation

# ADDITIONAL WORKS
# BY AUTHOR

## Sacrament of the Forest
How to become a Guardian of the Forest

# ADDITIONAL WORKS
# BY AUTHOR

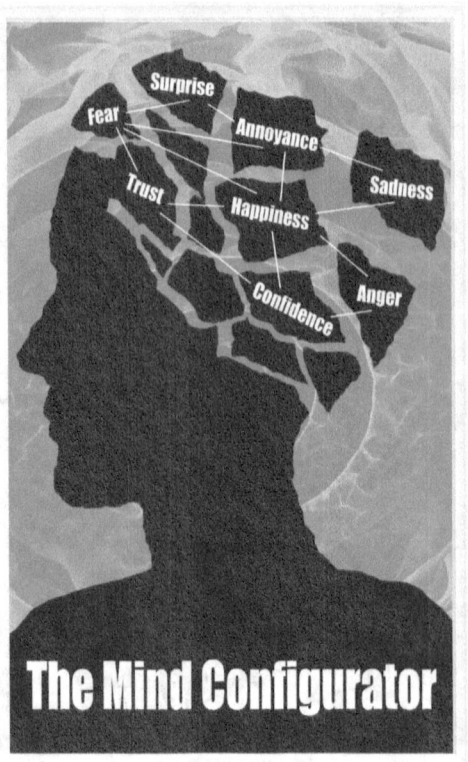

## TheMind Configurator
### Advanced Technique to access the Subconscious Mind

# ADDITIONAL WORKS
# BY AUTHOR

## The Sacramentum
Tarot/Oracle Cards

www.ingramcontent.com/pod-product-compliance
Lightning Source LLC
Chambersburg PA
CBHW050910120626
46554CB00003B/1110